THE
HEART
OF THE
WOOD

THE
HEART
OF THE
WOOD

by Marguerite W. Davol · illustrated by Sheila Hamanaka

SIMON & SCHUSTER BOOKS FOR YOUNG READERS
Published by Simon & Schuster
New York · London · Toronto · Sydney · Tokyo · Singapore

SIMON & SCHUSTER BOOKS FOR YOUNG READERS
Simon & Schuster Building, Rockefeller Center
1230 Avenue of the Americas, New York, New York 10020
Text copyright © 1992 by Marguerite W. Davol
Illustrations copyright © 1992 by Sheila Hamanaka
All rights reserved including the right of reproduction
in whole or in part in any form.
SIMON & SCHUSTER BOOKS FOR YOUNG READERS
is a trademark of Simon & Schuster.
Designed by Lucille Chomowicz.
The text of this book was set in 16 point Cartier.
The illustrations were done in oil paints on bark paper.
Manufactured in the United States of America

10 9 8 7 6 5 4 3 2 1
Library of Congress Cataloging-in-Publication Data
Davol, Marguerite W.   The heart of the wood / by Marguerite W. Davol;
illustrated by Sheila Hamanaka.   Summary: A cumulative tale
in which a tree that is home to a singing mockingbird continues
to be a source of music after it is fashioned into a fiddle.   [1. Stories in rhyme.
2. Music—Fiction. 3. Violins—Fiction.]   I. Hamanaka, Sheila, ill.   II. Title.
PZ8.3.D294He   1992   [E]—dc20   CIP   91-33742   ISBN 0-671-74778-9

To the generations of Gorse children,
who have challenged me and inspired me—MWD

To Hudson and Hemingway—SH

This is the tree, the sycamore tree, that grows
in the Winderly Woods.

This is the mockingbird perched in the tree
that grows in the Winderly Woods.

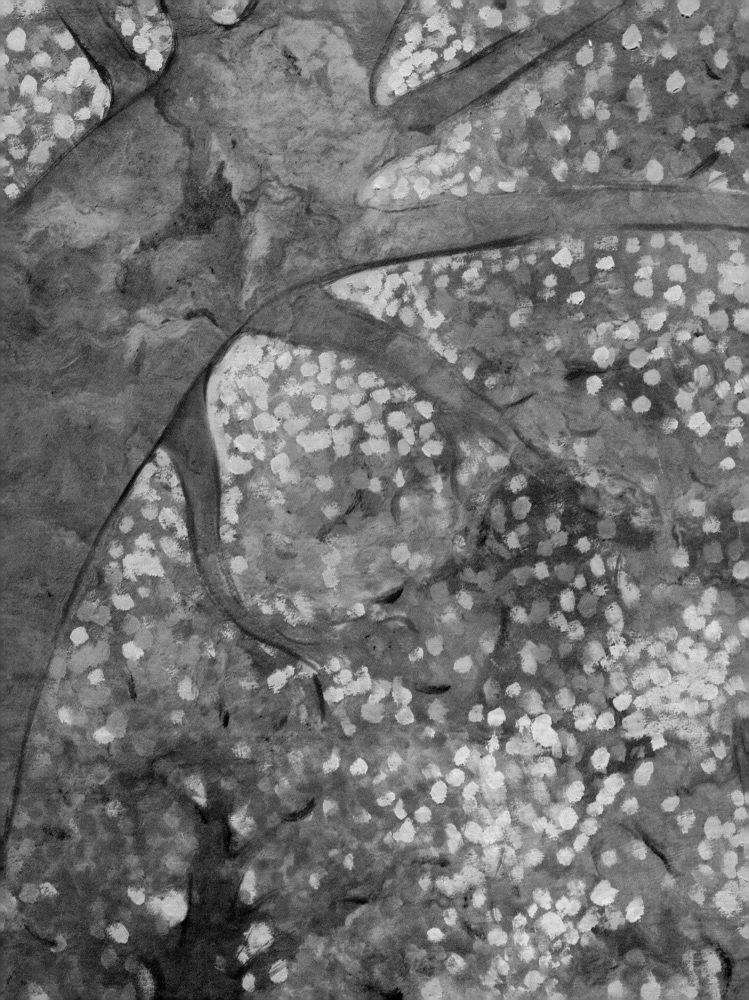

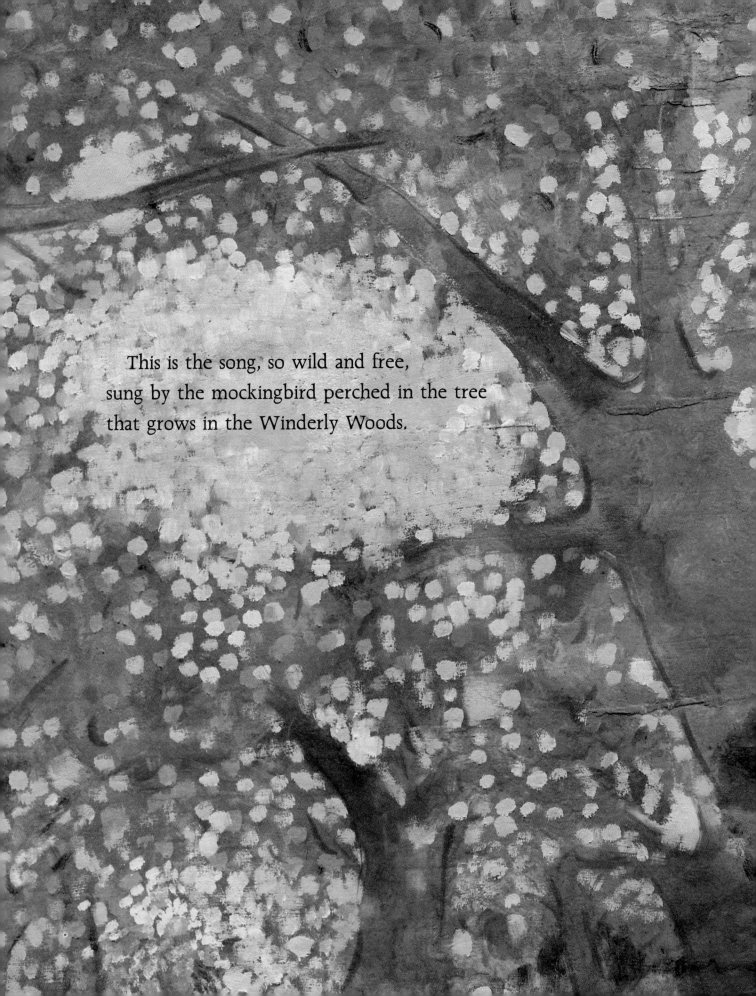

This is the song, so wild and free,
sung by the mockingbird perched in the tree
that grows in the Winderly Woods.

This is the woodcutter, sunburned and lean,
who heard the song, so wild and free,
sung by the mockingbird perched in the tree
that grows in the Winderly Woods.

This is the ax, sharpened and keen,
swung by the woodcutter, sunburned and lean,
who heard the song, so wild and free,
sung by the mockingbird perched in the tree
that grows in the Winderly Woods.

This is the tree trunk, toppled and still,
felled by the ax, sharpened and keen,
swung by the woodcutter, sunburned and lean,
who heard the song, so wild and free,
sung by the mockingbird perched in the tree
that grew in the Winderly Woods.

This is the sawmill, noisy and shrill,
trimming the tree trunk, toppled and still,
felled by the ax, sharpened and keen,
swung by the woodcutter, sunburned and lean,
who heard the song, so wild and free,
sung by the mockingbird perched in the tree
that grew in the Winderly Woods.

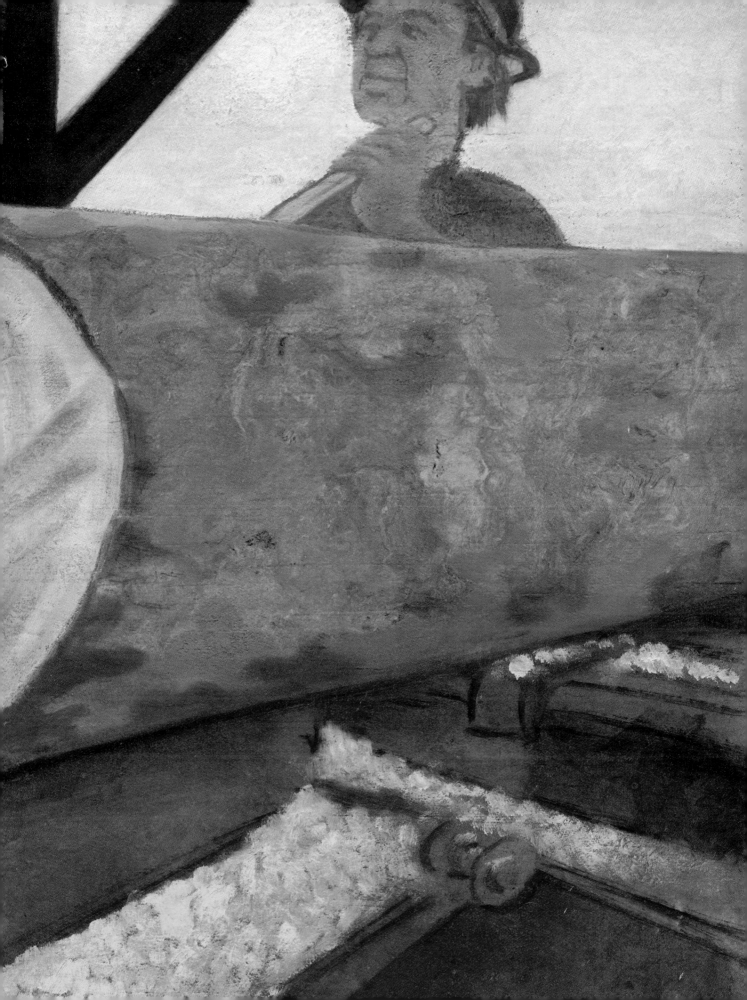

This is the woodcarver with music in mind
who shaped the heart of the wood,
the wood from the sawmill, noisy and shrill,
that trimmed the tree, toppled and still,
felled by the ax, sharpened and keen,
held by the woodcutter, sunburned and lean,
who heard the song, so wild and free,
sung by the mockingbird perched in the tree
that grew in the Winderly Woods.

This is the fiddle created to find
the song in the heart of the wood,
shaped by the woodcarver with music in mind
out of wood from the sawmill, noisy and shrill,
that trimmed the tree, toppled and still,
felled by the ax, sharpened and keen,
held by the woodcutter, sunburned and lean,
who heard the song, so wild and free,
sung by the mockingbird perched in the tree
that grew in the Winderly Woods.

This is the fiddler with fingers and bow,
playing the fiddle created to find
the song in the heart of the wood,
shaped by the woodcarver with music in mind
out of wood from the sawmill, noisy and shrill,
that trimmed the tree, toppled and still,
felled by the ax, sharpened and keen,
held by the woodcutter, sunburned and lean,
who heard the song, so wild and free,
sung by the mockingbird perched in the tree
that grew in the Winderly Woods.

This is the music, now high, now low,
made by the fiddler with fingers and bow,
playing the fiddle created to find
the song in the heart of the wood,

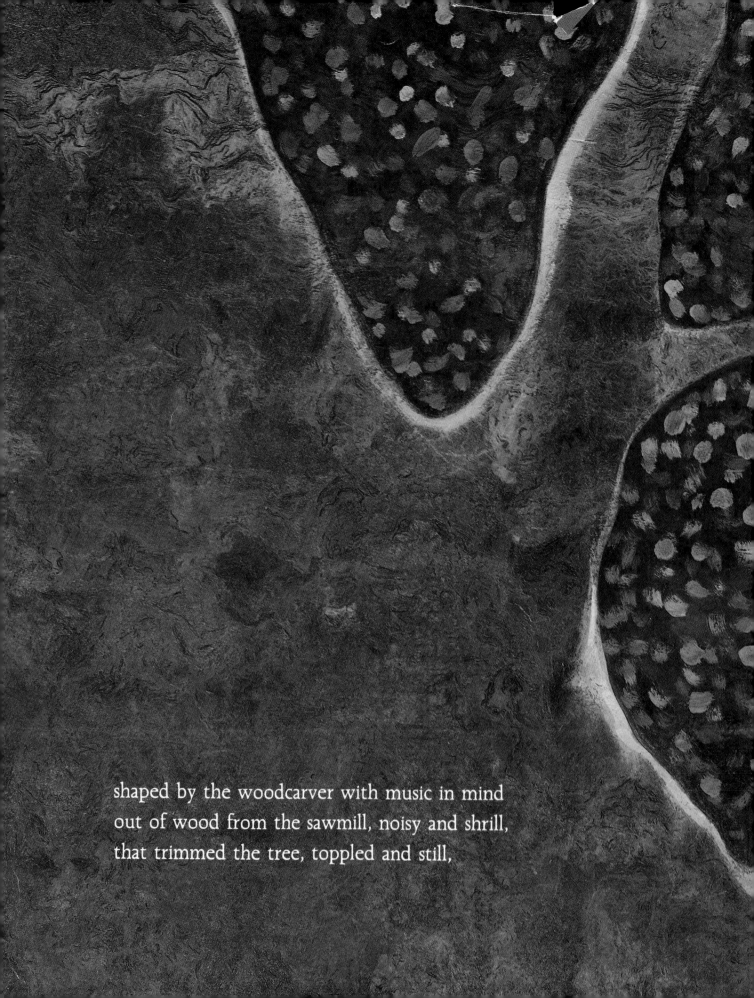

shaped by the woodcarver with music in mind
out of wood from the sawmill, noisy and shrill,
that trimmed the tree, toppled and still,

felled by the ax, sharpened and keen,
held by the woodcutter, sunburned and lean,
who heard the song, so wild and free,
sung by the mockingbird perched in the tree

that grew in the Winderly Woods.

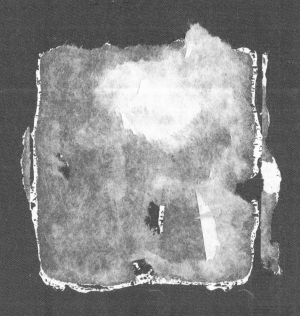